DISNEY
FROZEN

publications international, ltd.

When Princess Anna first discovers her sister Elsa's magical power, she thinks it's wonderful! Look around to find these icy things the two sisters made:

this igloo

snow angel

this flurry of snow

this sledding hill

pyramid of snowballs

Olaf the snowman

After Elsa accidentally puts a white streak in Anna's hair, the king worries she may hurt her little sister. Elsa decides to stay away from Anna to keep her safe. Look around for these things that Anna would like to share with her sister:

ice cream cones

dollhouse

jump rope

chess game

wishbone

these dolls

People from all over the world have come to Arendelle to attend Elsa's coronation. Find the charming Prince Hans and other visitors:

Once the townspeople see Elsa's icy magic, they become frightened. To avoid hurting someone with her powers, Elsa runs away. As she flees, look around the courtyard for these frozen creations:

this flag

icy lantern

this fountain

this topiary

this topiary

this stone

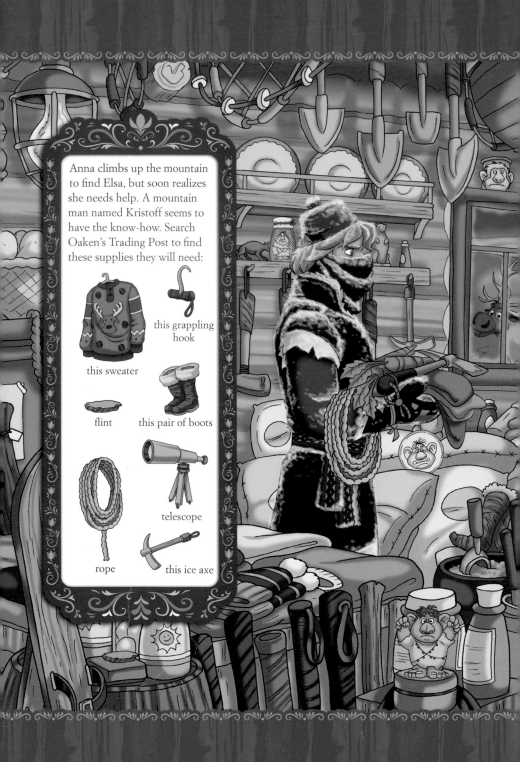

Anna climbs up the mountain to find Elsa, but soon realizes she needs help. A mountain man named Kristoff seems to have the know-how. Search Oaken's Trading Post to find these supplies they will need:

this sweater

this grappling hook

flint

this pair of boots

telescope

rope

this ice axe

Kristoff agrees to help Anna, but soon wonders whether that was a good idea! While they flee the wolves, look for Kristoff's scattered belongings:

scorched blanket

broken lute

sweater

sock

hat

mitten

Anna finds her sister and asks
Elsa to come home. But it will
take some convincing to get
Elsa to agree. As Elsa creates a
snowman named Marshmallow,
look for these other icy items
she has made:

Summer has finally returned to Arendelle! To thank Kristoff for helping her, Anna gives him a brand-new sled and some carrots for Sven. Look around town for these other things that Sven might need:

halter

water bucket

apple

snow goggles

blanket

snowshoes

Return to the two young sisters to find these decorations for a snowman:

carrot for nose

this lump of coal

branch for arm

these mittens

big button

this winter hat

Skip back to the scenes of the sisters growing up and search for these things:

knitting needles

yo-yo

guitar

book

tricycle

swing

Go back to the Arendelle docks to find these supplies:

this crate of apples

wheel of cheese

this crate of potatoes

bale of hay

sack of flour

barrel of pickled herring

As Elsa flees Arendelle, look for these frightened townspeople:

Go back to Oaken's Trading Post to find these troll souvenirs:

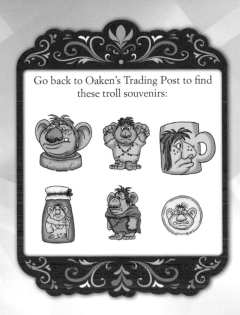

Run back to the wolves and find these animal tracks:

bear

moose

arctic fox

musk ox

beaver

horse

Return to Elsa's ice palace to find these frozen creations:

Search the streets of Arendelle to find these six pairs of sisters:

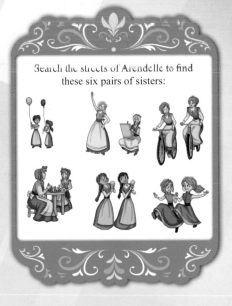